Vacation Day!

adapted by **Maggie Testa**

Simon Spotlight

New York   London   Toronto   Sydney   New Delhi

SIMON SPOTLIGHT
An imprint of Simon & Schuster Children's Publishing Division
1230 Avenue of the Americas, New York, New York 10020
This Simon Spotlight paperback edition May 2020
DreamWorks The Boss Baby: Back in Business © 2020 DreamWorks Animation LLC. All Rights Reserved.
All rights reserved, including the right of reproduction in whole or in part in any form.
SIMON SPOTLIGHT and colophon are registered trademarks of Simon & Schuster, Inc.
For information about special discounts for bulk purchases, please contact Simon & Schuster Special Sales at 1-866-506-1949 or
business@simonandschuster.com. Manufactured in the United States of America 0421 LAK
2 3 4 5 6 7 8 9 10 • ISBN 978-1-5344-6785-9 • ISBN 978-1-5344-6786-6 (eBook)

Boss Baby and Tim were going on a family vacation to Paris! Tim was so excited that he wasn't even nervous for the eight-hour airplane flight.

Boss Baby, though, wasn't so sure that the flight would be a breeze.

Boss Baby looked around the plane. There were babies everywhere. Then Marsha Krinkle and her cameraman from the Channel 8 news team boarded the plane. This was bad. Very bad.

"A transatlantic flight is a baby's worst nightmare!" Boss Baby explained to Tim. "Stuck in a seat for eight hours with air pressure hammering our sensitive eardrums means a guaranteed meltdown."

"Ugh, a crying baby on an airplane is the worst," Tim agreed.

"And that's just one baby," explained his brother. "We have thirteen on this flight. When one baby cries, it starts a chain reaction. Thirteen babies shrieking and wailing on a plane will be a news story that Marsha Krinkle won't be able to resist. The story will go global. One bad flight could make the whole world hate babies!"

"It's going to be okay," Tim said. All the moms and dads would make sure their babies didn't cry!

Then Boss Baby and Tim's parents put headphones over their ears. "Ooh, mellow saxophone jams," their mom said. Boss Baby and Tim watched as their parents fell fast asleep.

Soon everyone on the plane was asleep, except the babies and the grown-ups without babies . . . which included the Channel 8 news team!

Boss Baby was in a panic. At any moment, the babies could start crying. It would annoy all the passengers and decrease baby love!

Tim offered Boss Baby a bottle to help him calm down. Boss Baby began to drink his milk, but that only made him fall asleep! The plane began to take off. Tim was on his own!

It wasn't long before the babies began to whimper. Tim knew that it would turn into all-out screeching if he didn't act fast.

Tim jumped out of his seat and ran to a baby. It was Jimbo, and he was kicking the seat in front of him.

"Jimbo, you're bothering people and making other babies cry too," Tim said.

Jimbo frowned. "I can't help it. My ears hurt."

Tim gave Jimbo a bottle. Sucking on it made Jimbo's ears feel better!

After that, Tim went around the plane giving every baby a bottle or their pacifier. They all started to calm down.

There was one baby who didn't need any help: Staci. She and Tim were trying to figure things out when the flight attendant appeared. He walked Tim back to his seat.

"There we go. Snug and safe," the flight attendant said. "Are we going to sit like a good boy all the way to Paris?"

"Yes, sir," replied Tim.

"And will there be consequences if we don't?" the flight attendant asked.

"Yes, sir," sighed Tim. How would he help the babies now?

Soon Tim heard a baby start to cry again.

"Row 17," Staci told him through an earpiece. "Go help him. I'll watch out for the flight attendant."

Tim ran back to the crying baby. He searched around the baby's seat for his pacifier, but he couldn't find it anywhere!

"Try singing the baby a lullaby," suggested Staci. Tim didn't know any lullabies, so he started making up words to the tune of "Twinkle, Twinkle, Little Star."

"Baby rides a shiny airplane on a unicorn . . . made out of hugs," Tim sang. "Before the sleep unicorn comes for more hugs."

He knew it didn't make any sense, but the baby fell back asleep. He did it!

But Tim didn't have time to celebrate. The flight attendant found Tim and ordered him back to his seat. If he got up again, he'd be strapped into the jump seat with no way to escape!

A little while later, Tim was sitting quietly in his seat when Staci screamed into his earpiece, "The babies are all over the cabin!"

As the plane hit a few bumps, some of the babies started to cry. Soon they were all crying! Marsha Krinkle asked her cameraman to set up his equipment. She would call this news report "Flightmare"!

Tim had to get the babies back to their seats now. Staci would stay on the lookout for the flight attendant.

With some hustle and a little improvisation, Tim got all of the babies to calm down once again.

And he even got back to his seat before the flight attendant saw him. But as soon as Tim looked behind him to find Staci, he found the flight attendant instead!

"Busted!" the flight attendant cried. Tim was going to the jump seat and there was nothing he could do about it!

Boss Baby woke up for a second and started to laugh. "My pain is not funny," Tim told him.

With an hour left in the flight, Tim was stuck. He was strapped into the jump seat and there was no way out . . . until Boss Baby, still half asleep, started playing with the buckle on the jump seat. He miraculously freed Tim!

Tim ran over to the flight attendant and trapped him in a life vest. Now the flight attendant couldn't get in the way of Tim helping babies!

"We won! It's over!" Tim cheered, but Staci wasn't so sure. There was still a half hour left in the flight.

Suddenly they heard a loud noise. Startled, Jimbo started to cry. Soon all the other babies were crying—even Staci!

Marsha Krinkle and her cameraman set up their equipment and were about to start filming. Tim had to think of something fast. And that's when he accidentally fell against the back of a seat, and one of the crying babies started giggling.

"I know how to fix this," Tim said. "And it's going to hurt."

Tim purposely got the attention of the flight attendant, who had just wriggled out of the life vest. He knew the flight attendant would chase him around the plane until Tim was sitting in his seat again.

As Tim and the flight attendant ran around the plane, Tim tripped, fell, and ran into things. With each fall, more and more babies started giggling. "My pain is funny," he told them.

By the time Marsha Krinkle's camera was rolling, the babies were all laughing and happy. Tim had saved the world's love for babies!

When Boss Baby woke up, he thanked Tim. "You've done Baby Corp. a great service today."

"It was teamwork," Tim replied, looking up at Staci.

Now it was time to take a vacation day. Tim had earned it!